If
you take
a careful look,
you'll see
how
creatures
in this book
are
CAMOUFLAGED
and out
of view—
although
they're
right
in
front
of
you.

how to hide a polar bear

& OTHER MAMMALS

BY RUTH HELLER

Grosset & Dunlap

Copyright © 1985 by Ruth Heller. All rights reserved. Published by Grosset & Dunlap, a member of The Putnam Publishing Group, New York. Printed in Italy. Published simultaneously in Canada. Library of Congress Catalog Card Number 85-70286   ISBN 0-448-10477-6   A B C D E F G H I J

A
POLAR BEAR
will only go
where there is
lots of ice
and snow.

Its fur is
always white,
you know,
so it will
hardly…

even
show.

The
SHOWSHOE HARE
is turning brown
because the snow is melting down,
and
when there's only snow in patches
you will find that this hare...

matches.

This
dappled DEER
will
disappear
into the
filtered
sunlight…

here.

A
ZEBRA
doesn't
seem
to be
a creature
who hides easily,
but in the shade,
behind a tree,
its
silhouette
is…

hard
to
see.

The
lazy
LEOPARD
likes
to lie
upon a
leafy limb,
where leaves
and bark
and sunshine
and
his spots
have…

hidden
him.

The color of the
   LION
and the color
of his mane
and the color
of the grass
that grows
upon the
plain
all...

seem
to be the
same.

Because
the
SLOTH's
so
very
slow,
green algae
find
the time
to
grow and thrive
upon its
thick
coarse
hair.

Then
you can
hardly
tell...

it's
there.